Stan Lee presents:

# SPIDER-MAN
# FEARFUL SYMMETRY:
# KRAVEN'S LAST HUNT

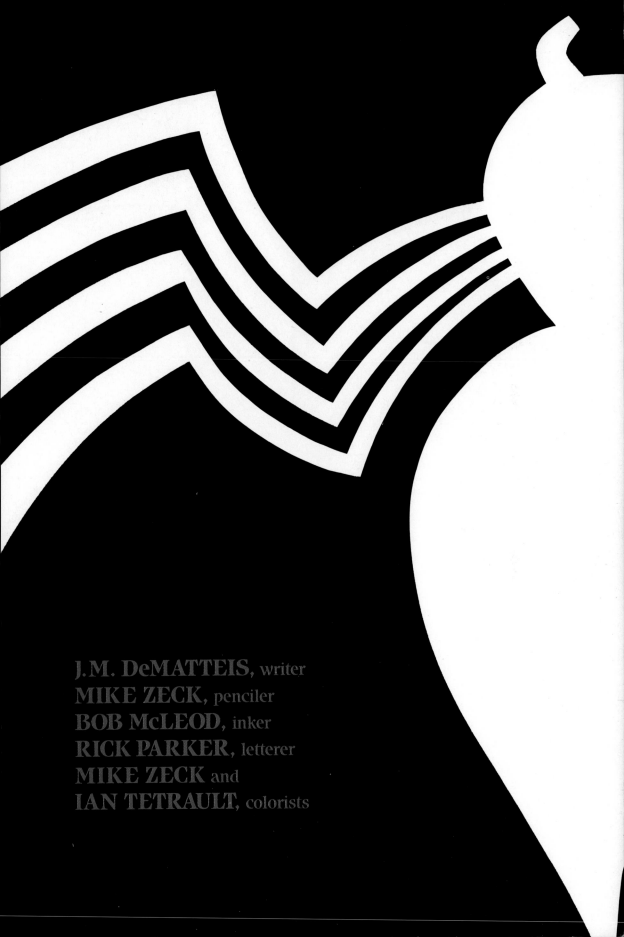

J.M. DeMATTEIS, writer
MIKE ZECK, penciler
BOB McLEOD, inker
RICK PARKER, letterer
MIKE ZECK and
IAN TETRAULT, colorists

Dedicated, with much love, to Meherabad's resident
comic book maven, **Jack C. Small**. Jai Baba!
—J. M. D.

Dedicated to **Stan** and **Steve** who had the power
to turn me into a comics fan for life.
—M. Z.

Dedicated to **Neal Adams**, who got
me my first job in comics
and inspired me to learn
how to do it right.
—B. M.

**Tom DeFalco**
Editor in Chief

**Jim Salicrup**
Editor

**Glenn Herdling**
Associate Editor

**Dawn Geiger** and **Mike Zeck**
Designers

**Virginia Romita**
Traffic/Production Manager

**Alison Gill**
Manufacturing Coordinator

**Jack Abel**
Proofreader

Kraven logo designed
by **Ken Lopez**

**THE AMAZING SPIDER-MAN®** Fearful Symmetry: Kraven's Last Hunt™.
Originally published in magazine form as Web of Spider-Man #32, 33,
Amazing Spider-Man #293, 294, Spectacular Spider-Man #131, 132.
Published by Marvel Comics, 387 Park Avenue South, New York, N.Y.
10016. Copyright © 1989, 1990 by Marvel Entertainment Group, Inc.
All rights reserved. SPIDER-MAN, KRAVEN and all prominent
characters appearing herein and the distinctive names and likenesses
thereof are trademarks of Marvel Entertainment Group, Inc. No part of
this book may be printed or reproduced in any manner without the
written permission of the publisher.

Printed in the U.S.A.              First Trade Paperback Printing.
ISBN # 0-87135-691-0

Cover art by **Mike Zeck** and **Phil Zimelman**

# Introduction

Let's be honest.

Writing an introduction for someone is usually a bore. You do it if that someone is a good friend and twists your arm, but even then you usually do it reluctantly.

Not in this case, Charlie!

The first time I read this six-part literary and artistic bombshell pitting Spidey against Kraven in (literally) a battle to the death, with Vermin almost stealing the show, I knew I had just been privy to a classic in the making. I also knew that fans everywhere would soon clamor for that incredible saga to be re-published as a graphic novel, for it certainly deserves a place of honor on any library bookshelf.

That's why, when Editor Jim Salicrup asked me to write the intro for this intensely dramatic tale, I leapt at the opportunity. In fact, my only shred of reluctance is caused by the fear that I may not be able to do justice to so remarkable an epic.

Perhaps the first thing you'll notice when you start to read Part One, "The Coffin," is the fact that you're doing more than reading it, you'll feel as though you're actually living it. Credit this to the amazingly vivid literary style employed by the brilliant J.M. DeMatteis, a style that carries you along with the action as if you're somehow inside the heart and mind of each of our tortured characters.

And tortured they are, hero and villain alike. But so finely honed are DeMatteis's depictions of Peter, Kraven, and Vermin that the words "hero" and "villain" seem woefully inadequate. For, on the pages that follow, you'll find no mere one-dimensional good guys and bad guys to cheer for and revile. No, thanks to DeMatteis's skill and sensitivity, each character is so delicately shaded, so perceptively fine-tuned that even the villains will get a stranglehold on your emotions.

But take it from a guy who's worked with many of the finest illustrators ever to come down the pike, no matter how good a story may be, the artwork can make it or break it. And never has artwork more gloriously complemented a script than here, in the case of Mike Zeck's magnificent, totally awesome penciling.

Starting with the very first title illustration, the masterfully menacing rendition of a naked Kraven crouching, about to attack, Mike's artwork never falters. His compositions, his characters' expressions, his action scenes have an almost hypnotic effect upon the reader, an effect that captures your attention immediately and never seems to let you go.

One word that continually comes to mind is "realism." Each panel penciled by Mike seems to be torn from life. No matter how outrageous the situation, you find yourself believing it. You have to believe it, it looks so real. As the pages unfold, you'll be aware of the stench of the sewers, the mold of the graves. Such is the talent of Mike Zeck that you'll share the fear and the rage in Peter Parker's heart; you'll understand the mayhem and the majesty that is Sergei Kravinoff; you may even find a strange compassion for the mindless violence and tragic madness of the creature called Vermin.

For here you will find no clichéd cardboard characters, no trite and time-tested stereotypes. Thanks to the genius of DeMatteis and Zeck, everyone you'll encounter in this pulse-pounding tale will live and breathe, surprise you and startle you, as shock follows shock, carrying you along on a journey into drama that you'll never forget.

But even though I know how eager you are to get started, I cannot omit the third member of the talented triumverate that has brought you this true Marvel masterwork. Just as the artist must glorify the writer's script, so must the inker glorify the artist's penciled drawings. And never has the word glorify been more accurately used than in the case of Bob McLeod's magnificent renderings. In fact, Bob has done far more than just ink over Mike's pencils. Bob has acted as a creative partner, embellishing each illustration, giving it the sheen, the brilliance, the rich, moody quality which makes it almost obligatory to re-publish this saga in permanent, hardcover form.

I've been with Spidey for many years. Didn't think there was much that could excite me or surprise me in the way of new and different stories. But every so often I see a special issue, fantastically written, magnificently illustrated, and dazzlingly conceived. This is one of those times.

Yes, I'm delighted to have been asked to write this introduction. There's only one thing that bugs me...

I'm jealous of DeMatteis, Zeck, and McLeod.

Excelsior!

# CHAPTER

# 1

# THE COFFIN

--the beast.

My mind is rage and glory.

My heart is fire and pride.

My body is grace and power.

I am Kravinov--

SHUK

12

--the *man*.

An *old* man, now--'though few would believe it.

Just a *child* when my parents came to this country, shortly after the overthrow of the Czar--some seventy odd years ago.

There was no more *room* in Russia for aristocrats. For culture. For *honor*.

For human dignity.

But all those things were bred in my bones, long before the Trotskys and Lenins dragged my homeland into the pit.

Dignity? Honor? Where are such qualities today? All the *world*, it seems, has followed Russia's sad example.

Were my parents alive today, they would look upon this frightened, wounded animal called civilization without recognition--and with great *fear*.

And great *disgust*.

I am *KRAVEN*--

--the *HUNTER.*

I have found dignity, not in the cities, but in the jungles.

I have found honor, not in the civilized, but in the *primal.*

I have found morality, I have found *meaning* --in the *hunt.*

But I cannot escape Time forever. Herbs and roots and potions cannot rejuvenate a dying spirit--or heal a heart crushed by the weight of a corrupted Age.

I will die soon. I *must* die soon.

*But not yet.*

JOE FACE IS DEAD.

WHY SHOULD I CARE.

HE WAS JUST ANOTHER STREET-SNITCH... A TWO-BIT THUG. SOMETIMES I'D PUMP HIM FOR INFORMATION AND SOMETIMES I'D PUT HIM AWAY.

AND NOW HE'S DEAD.

SO WHY SHOULD I CARE?

HOW MANY JOE FACES HAVE I KNOWN OVER THE YEARS? TOO MANY TO COUNT. THEY'RE NOT PEOPLE. THEY'RE OBSTACLES IN MY WAY. MEANS TO AN END.

AND, IF THEY DIE...

POOR, STUPID SAP--

SORRY, WE'RE CLOSED!

...WHY SHOULD I CARE?

DIDN'T LEAVE BEHIND NO MONEY, NO FAM'LY TA SPEAK OF.

WE'RE ALL YA HAD, JOEY.

AN' THIS IS THE BEST WE COULD DO.

SHUK SHUK SHUK

WE GOT UP A *COLLECTION* FOR YA, *JOEY*. FIGURED THE LEAST WE OWED YA WAS A DECENT BOX AN' A PIECE O' GROUND.

YEAH. AN' MAYBE SOMEDAY...SOME-BODY'LL DO THE SAME FOR--

*KREEEEEEK*

...US...

HOLY JEEZ, IT'S--

*SPIDER-MAN.*

BUT THEY CAN'T QUITE GET THE *NAME* OUT OF THEIR MOUTHS.

*THEY'RE TOO SCARED.*

RUNNING FROM SOMEONE WHO DOESN'T EVEN EXIST.

JOE FACE WAS SCARED, TOO. HE USED TO *SHAKE* WHEN HE'D SEE ME. HE USED TO RUN--JUST LIKE *THEY'RE* RUNNING.

THERE *IS* NO SPIDER-MAN. HE'S A MASK. A *MYTH.*

*OPEN*

*THWIP!*

STOP!! I DIDN'T COME LOOKING FOR TROUBLE!

A LIE.

OH, SURE, IT'D BE GREAT IF PUTTING ON A COSTUME COULD MIRACULOUSLY *CHANGE* THE MAN UNDERNEATH. BUT IT *CAN'T.* I'M *NOT* SPIDER-MAN.

I'M JUST... PETER PARKER.

I CAME TO SAY GOODBYE.

AND I GUESS I DO CARE.

BUT THEY'LL NEVER UNDERSTAND THAT. HOW COULD THEY? HOW COULD ANYBODY?

SOMETIMES I WISH I COULD GET INTO THEIR HEADS... SEE MYSELF THE WAY THEY SEE ME.

HARRY, NO--!

YOU KIDDIN'? I NAIL THAT WALL-CRAWLIN' FREAK AN' MY REP'S MADE IN THIS TOWN!

ON SECOND THOUGHT -- MAYBE NOT.

DON'T

EVEN

TRY.

GOOD BOY, HARRY. SKITTER OFF INTO A CORNER AND HIDE.

WOULDN'T WANT TO GET TOO CLOSE TO THE "WALL-CRAWLING FREAK," WOULD YOU?

WOULDN'T WANT TO FIND OUT THAT HE'S AS HUMAN AS YOU ARE?

A DECENT BOX AND A PIECE OF GROUND.

AS FRAGILE?

SHUK

AS SCARED OF DYING?

THAT'S WHAT THIS IS ALL ABOUT, ISN'T IT?

YESTERDAY, NED LEEDS. TODAY, JOE FACE. TOMORROW...

AUNT MAY? MARY JANE?

ME?

FUNNY. I'M OUT THERE FACING DEATH EVERY DAY AS SPIDER-MAN--BUT I NEVER REALLY THINK ABOUT IT. GUESS I DON'T LET MYSELF.

YET SO MANY PEOPLE I LOVE HAVE DIED BE- FORE THEIR TIME: UNCLE BEN, CAPTAIN STACY, GWEN-- NOW NED...

DO I THINK I'M SOMEHOW IMMUNE?

I'M GOING TO DIE.

CLICK

BUT NOT YET.

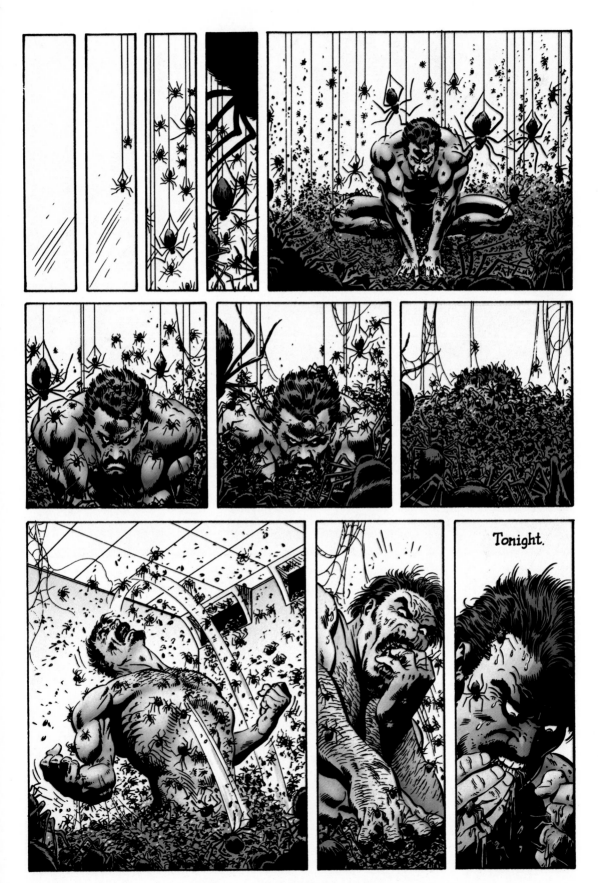

Tonight.

HEAD'S POUNDING--

--LIKE SOMEONE'S PLAYING DRUMS INSIDE MY BRAIN. *JUNGLE* DRUMS.

GOT THE SHIVERS. STOMACH'S IN A KNOT. MAYBE I'LL JUST CRAWL UP INTO A BALL AND--

NO.

JUST KEEP MOVING. GOTTA KEEP MOVING--AND EVERY-THING'LL BE ALL RIGHT.

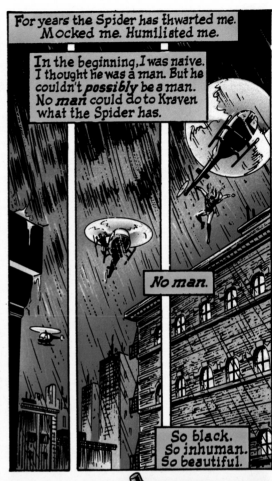

For years the Spider has thwarted me. Mocked me. Humiliated me.

In the beginning, I was naive. I thought he was a man. But he couldn't *possibly* be a man. No *man* could do to Kraven what the Spider has.

*No man.*

So black. So inhuman. So beautiful.

You exist to *test* me, don't you? To taunt and challenge me?

And I cannot rest until I have proven myself. Until I have *destroyed* you--

*I cannot rest.*

SHUK

OKAY, PARKER-- LET'S GET REAL.

EVER SINCE NED DIED, YOU'VE BEEN UPSET. REALLY UPSET.

SO

THAT'S TO BE EXPECTED. THAT'S NORMAL.

SO WHY

AND WHAT YOU'RE FEELING NOW... IT'S NOT SURPRISING. YOU HAVEN'T BEEN SLEEPING WELL. YOU'VE BEEN ON THE MOVE CONSTANTLY.

AND SEEING JOE FACE TONIGHT DIDN'T HELP THINGS ANY.

SO WHY AM I SO SURE THAT

YOUR NERVES ARE SHOT. YOU'RE DOG-TIRED. YOU'RE PROBABLY COMING DOWN WITH THE FLU.

aid

KILLS BUGS DEAD

ERE THEY HIDE!

SO WHY AM I SO SURE THAT SOMETHING'S OUT THERE.

THAT SOMETHING'S WAITING FOR ME.

SHUK SHUK SHUK

Spyder! Spyder! burning bright

In the forests of the night,

What immortal hand or eye

Could frame thy fearful symmetry?

FUT!

DUMB. VERY DUMB.

MY SPIDER-SENSE WARNED ME IN TIME. I SHOULD HAVE BEEN ABLE TO DODGE THAT SECOND DART. BUT I WAS SLOPPY. NO--

DART?

--I WAS--

DART?

--SCARED.

DART?

OF COURSE!!

IT'S GOTTA BE HIM!

23

JOE FACE.

NO...IT CAN'T BE! HE'S DEAD!

JOE FACE.

THAT DART... MUST'VE BEEN TIPPED WITH... I DUNNO...SOME KIND OF DRUG OR POTION, OR...

JOE FACE.

IT'S NOT JOE FACE! IT'S--

KRAVEN!

Come to me, Spider.

Tonight I have widened my consciousness with herbs and roots. Tonight I have *immersed* myself in your being... eaten of your flesh.

Tonight my mind has *penetrated* your essence. It *feasts* upon you, like maggots feasting upon a corpse.

Come to me.

IT'SNOTJOEFACEIT'S KRAVENIT'SNOTJOEFACE IT'S KRAVENIT'SNOT JOEFACEIT'S--

KRAVEN... IT WON'T WORK.

COME TO ME, SPIDER--

--AND LET HONOR BE RESTORED!

THWAK!

THAT'S TWICE I LET HIM CATCH ME. WHAT THE DEVIL'S WRONG WITH ME?

MUSCLES ARE GETTING STIFF.

I CAN HARDLY LIFT MY HEAD.

OH, HE'S DRUGGED ME, ALL RIGHT. BUT IF I CAN JUST HANG IN FOR A LITTLE WHILE, MY RECUPERATIVE POWERS SHOULD THROW OFF THE EFFECTS BEFORE TOO--

25

TERRIFIC.

DON'T KNOW WHAT THIS NET IS MADE OF-- BUT IT'S SOMETHING I'D HAVE TROUBLE WITH AT FULL STRENGTH.

HEADACHE'S GETTING WORSE.

AND THE WAY I'M FEELING NOW, IT COULD TAKE ME ALL NIGHT--

DRUMS.

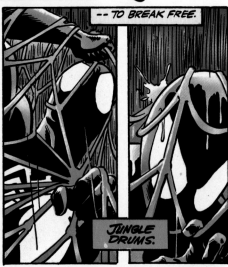

-- TO BREAK FREE.

JUNGLE DRUMS.

OKAY, SO MAYBE IT WILL TAKE ALL NIGHT.

I'VE BEEN IN WORSE SHAPE BEFORE. I KNOW KRAVEN'S METHOD.

WHAT'S THAT HE'S GOT THERE?

HE'S JUST LIKE DOC OCK AND THE VULTURE AND ALL THE REST OF 'EM.

LOOKS LIKE A RIFLE.

HE'S

YESTERDAY, NED LEEDS.

OUT

TODAY, JOE FACE.

OF

TOMORROW

HIS

AUNT MAY? MARY JANE?

BLAM

SHUK SHUK

30

KRA-KOOM!

SHUK

CHUD

Spyder! Spyder! burning bright

In the forests of the night

What immortal hand or eye

Could frame thy fearful

symmetry?

31

# CHAPTER

# 2

# CRAWLING

HA-HA-HA!

yum.

HERE LIES
SPIDER-MAN

SLAIN BY
THE HUNTER

they're ssso ssstrange... the onesss that live *up there.*

look at thisss one... with her funny clothesss and sssweet sssmell.

i don't remember how they do that... make themssselves sssmell like that... like...

perfume. i think that's what they call it. a masssk in a bottle.

not a very *good* mask, though.

W-WHO'S THERE?

she'sss jusst like *all* of them up there. underneath the sssweet sssmell isss a ssstink worssse than *mine.*

but, oh, how they like to pretend they're *better* than me.

WHO'S--?

it'sss becaussse of them that I have to *hide* down here.

OH MY GOD!

them. and their funny clothesss. and their sweet smellsss.

MY NAME ISSS *VERMIN.*

yum. yum. yum.

38

SOMEHOW, I THOUGHT BEING A NEWLYWED WOULD BE A LITTLE DIFFERENT.

SITTING BY THE FIRE, DRINKING WHITE WINE... SNUGGLING UP...

BUT, OF COURSE, THAT REQUIRES SOMEONE TO SNUGGLE UP WITH. AND MY SOMEONE... MY HUSBAND... ISN'T HERE.

WHERE ARE YOU, PETER? YOU WERE SUPPOSED TO MEET ME HERE HOURS AGO AND HELP ME PACK UP THE REST OF MY STUFF, GET IT OVER TO YOUR... OUR... PLACE.

BUT, NO, YOU'RE PROBABLY OUT THERE WEBBING AROUND... MAKING THE WORLD FREE AND SAFE FOR DEMOCRACY... FIGHTING FOR YOUR LIFE AGAINST DOCTOR SQUID OR OCTOPUS OR WHATEVER HIS NAME IS!

YOU'RE PROBABLY...

...DEAD?!....

STOP THAT, MARY JANE! PETER'S BEEN PLAYING HERO SINCE HIGH SCHOOL. HE'S GOOD AT WHAT HE DOES. HE'S...

...DEAD?...

OH, GREAT!

SPEND A FORTUNE ON THESE MANHATTAN RENTS AND THIS IS WHAT YOU GET FOR YOUR MONEY.

FREEZE, YOU LITTLE--

PETER'S DEAD.

40

The Spider lies in a grave, a hundred miles from here. Down in the darkness. Blasted into oblivion.

*By my hand.*

My greatest enemy. My greatest tormentor. That black, hideous, *beautiful* beast.

*BY MY HAND.*

But it's not *enough* to simply destroy him. I must *become* him! I must prove myself *superior* to him --

-- and laugh in the face of his hovering ghost.

So now I see through the Spider's eyes. I wear the Spider's skin. I crawl.

Now--

*I am the Spider.*

THE HUNTER

41

No.

I am Kravinov, the man.

I am Kraven the hunter.

And my metamorphosis is not yet complete.

My metamorphosis.

Why.

I must merge with the Spider.

With its blasphemous sacred essence.

Why am I

With the horror and majesty at its core.

Why am I doing this?

Don't question: drink. Herbs and roots and juices; poisons, fruits, and flowers. Let them pervade your mind... widen it... shatter your Kravenness --

AYEEEEEE EE

-- and let in Spiderness. Let in--

Pain.

Why am I doing this?

For honor? (Pain!) For dignity? (Pain!) For all that your father bequeathed you?

PAIN.

My father! A pompous fool!... a Russian nobleman-- exiled and living in poverty in America; too attached to what was to ever see what is!

PAIN!

No. No! Father... Father was a god! The last remnant of a world of culture and decency.

A World the Spider CONSUMED.

YOU did it!

Russia was the model for a new and better -- a holy! -- civilization ...and you crushed it!

KRASH!

Just as you crushed my father!

My heart.

KRASH!

You take the guise of a Trotsky... a Lenin... a Hitler... a Reagan... a Gorbachev...

...a man in a mask: it makes no difference!

SHAKKK!

You crawl -- and the world becomes meaningless! You crawl -- and humankind tumbles into the pit!

YOU!

I AM

SPIDER!

I AM SO

COME OUT!

I AM SO AFRAID.

44

licklicklick the fingersss. goodygoodgood.

tough. tasty.

yum.

sssilly world up there. sssilly people. i hate 'em. i--

...i...

i know that...that...

what'sss it called?

newsss. newsss.

newsss-paper.

picturesss. and wordsss. i could think...no, tell... no, read the wordsss once. before. before.

before what? before i wasss? what wasss i before i wasss?

...what?!...

nonononononononono!!!

bad man... ...bad... veryvery bad!

crawly man. insect man.

spider-man.

he hurt me...yesterday? forever ago? today? hurtme hurtme hurtme.

him...and that other one... that nasssty sssoldier-man with the redwhite-blue. captain...flag? captain...

america.

isss that why i'm hiding? becausse of them?

i'm vermin! i'm not afraid of anyone! i'll rip thossse two to pieces! i'll chew 'em up!

no...i don't hide becaussse i'm afraid. i hide becaussse it'sss good to hide. becaysse when you hide in the dark no one can ssssee you or touch you or tell you what to do.

the dark isss warm and sssafe and ssstrong. jussst vermin and his sssquealing, dirty friendsss.

oh, but ssspiderman and captain america... i've got to show them.

show them that i'm not afraid!

sshow them that i can come up out of the dark...

...whenever...

...i...

KLANK

46

47

WHAT AM I DOING OUT HERE? IT'S THE MIDDLE OF THE NIGHT. DO I REALLY THINK I'LL FIND HIM?

GOD, THIS IS LIKE WHEN I WAS A KID AND I'D STAY OUT FIVE MINUTES PAST CURFEW AND MOM'D COME LOOKING FOR ME AND EMBARRASS ME IN FRONT OF MY FRIENDS!

TOK TOK TOK

I MEAN, WHAT AM I GOING TO SAY WHEN... IF... I FIND HIM?

"OH, SPIDER-MAN! YOU'VE BEEN OUT TOO LATE AND YOUR WIFE'S WORRIED!"

"AW, GEE, NOT NOW! I'M FIGHTING THE HOBGOBLIN!"

WHAT AM I DOING OUT HERE?!

OOO, I THINK I'M GONNA DIE! I NEVER SEEN ANYONE IN PANTS THAT TIGHT!

YEAH... AND THAT RED HAIR!

HEY, TIGHT-PANTS-- COME AND SHOW US YOUR RED HAIR!

THERE'S AN OLD LATIN PHRASE THAT APPLIES PERFECTLY TO THIS SITUATION. ...MAYBE YOU'VE HEARD IT--

"GET STUFFED!"

NOW THAT WAS SMART.

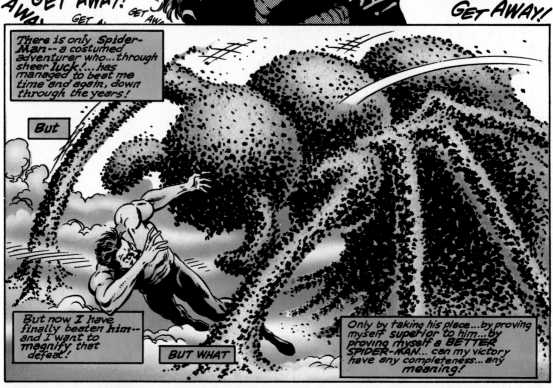

50

GET AWAY! IT'S TRUE! GET AWAY! IT'S TRUE! GET AWAY! IT'S TRUE! GET AWAY! IT'S TRUE! GET AWAY! IT'S TRUE!

Don't panic! Fear eats you! Fear murders you! Remember what you're doing!

GET AWAY! IT'S TRUE! GET AWAY! IT'S TRUE! GET AWAY! IT'S TRUE! GET AWAY! GET AWAY! IT'S TRUE! GET AWAY! IT'S TRUE!

Remember WHY!

To become spider-man... you must absorb the essence of spider-man... you must let in spider-ness... surrender to it!

I AM KRAVEN.

SSSpider-man.

...I...

SSSpider-man!!

KEEP WALKING, M.J.

DON'T LOOK BACK.

SHUT OFF YOUR MIND. SHUT OFF YOUR EARS.

YOU DON'T HEAR THEIR SNEAKERS SLAPPING THE PUDDLES.

SWAP

SWAP

SWAP YOU DON'T HEAR THEM GIGGLING LIKE CHIMPS IN HEAT.

OH, YES I DO!

I'M OUT OF HERE!

SWAP

SWAP

SSCARED.

GOTCHA!!

I'M DEAD.

they're ssscared. i can sssmell it.

but what are they ssscared of? each other? no -- sssomething elssse.

OKAY, MISS TIGHTPANTS! MISS REDHAIR! YOU'D BETTER--

i can sssmell it.

I'M DEAD. I'M--

HEY-- WHAT'RE YOU *SMILIN'* ABOUT?

OH--

-- SAVED.

-- NOTHING.

I am the spider.

SWAPPP

SKKRAAK

S-STOP
IT!

STOP!

I AM THE SPIDER.

THAT WASN'T PETER.

ssspider-man. that'sss why i came out. i have to... i have to...

i have to eat. i'm hungry. i'm alwaysss hungry.

no. i can eat later.

now i have to...

i'm not sure. do i have to follow him? or... or make him come to me?

doesssn't matter. not yet. i'm out-- that'sss what'sss important.

and i'm not afraid

not one bit.

don't know why i ssspent sso much time down there. hiding'sss sso ssstupid.

i'm hungry.

think i will find sssome food.

yum.

KRA-KOOM!

SPIDER-MAN

SLAIN BY

THE HUNTER

# CHAPTER
# 3

# DESCENT

I watch them through the glass: specimens. *Flies.* Watch them. I.

I am the Spider.

And I know.

In ways normal men cannot: *I know.*

I see into things; *beyond* things. I see the strands of Fate that bind us: victims to victor.

So let them scream; let them shout my name.

59

My ears hear nothing but the weaving of the web.

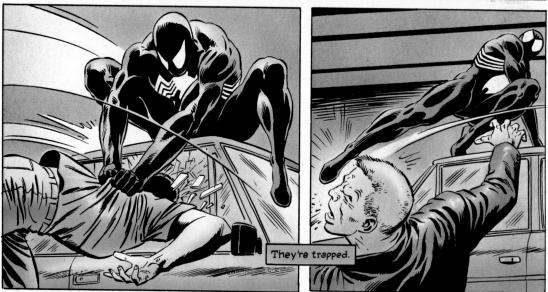

They're trapped.

And I devour them.

One game concludes, another *begins*:

They burst in, feigning shock, annoyance, fear.

Magnificent actors in a play of my creation.

They serve me; *worship* me. But the world must never know.

So I skitter into the night, while they "order" me to stop.

Skitter. I.

...GOT AWAY. *BLAST IT!*

LOOK ON THE BRIGHT SIDE-- HE SAVED US A WHOLE LOTTA *TROUBLE.* WE GOT EVERY LAST ONE OF THESE PUNKS.

--AND A HALF A MILLION IN *HEROIN*-- WITHOUT WORKING UP A SWEAT.

YEAH. TERRIFIC. SO HOW COME I'M NOT *HAPPY* ABOUT THAT?

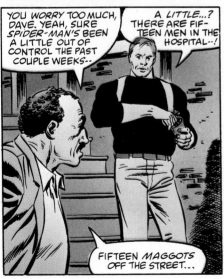

YOU *WORRY* TOO MUCH, DAVE. YEAH, SURE *SPIDER-MAN'S* BEEN A LITTLE OUT OF CONTROL THE PAST COUPLE WEEKS--

A *LITTLE...?* THERE ARE FIF- TEEN MEN IN THE HOSPITAL--!

FIFTEEN *MAGGOTS* OFF THE STREET...

THIS ONE AIN'T GOIN' T' ANY HOSPITAL, LIEUTENANT.

WHAT? WHY *NOT?*

HE'S *DEAD.*

I am the Spider.

No-- *not* the Spider.

**I AM KRAVEN!!**

I have slain the Spider. *Become* him.

I have hunted as the Spider hunts... consumed the Spider's prey.

I have proven myself his *superior* in every way. No-- *almost* every way. The *final* proof *comes*--

TAXI!

TAXI!

TAX--

SPLOOSH

YEAH. GREAT. THANKS A LOT.

JERK.

I'LL *WALK* IT'S ONLY TEN BLOCKS. IT'S ONLY POURING.

SO *WHAT* IF EVERYONE IN THE CITY'S SCARED TO DEATH BECAUSE *SPIDER-MAN* SEEMS TO HAVE LOST HIS MIND.

SO WHAT IF THERE'S A LUNATIC OUT ON THE STREETS *KILLING* PEOPLE AND THEN *EATING* THEM FOR BREAK--

--FAST ☀

yum.

blue sssuit. pale ssskin. big club. hithurthithurt hithurt hithurt.

NOW I'M HITTING BACK!!

WHUD!

beforebeforebefore: what wasss i before? i wasss small and dark and cold. i wasss hit and hurt andhurtand hit.

i wasss eaten alive.

i was a...a...a...

no! it doesssn't matter what i was before. now isss what matterssss. i'mverminver-min VERMIN!

i'm--

BLAM!

POLICE

65

...ALL RIGHT, YOU... J-JUST HOLD IT RIGHT THERE!

voice.

sssuch a prettypretty voice.

NOW YOU C-CALL OFF THOSE RATS--YOU *HEAR* ME? YOU CALL 'EM OFF!

seskin: ssso sssoft, ssso dark.

lipsss ssso full.

jussst like...

GO! LET HIM GO!

SKREE SKREE SKREE SKREE SKREE SKREE SKREE SKREE

jussst

THWAK!

like

CHUNG!

66

I SHOULDN'T BE DOING THIS. I SHOULDN'T BE COMING HERE.

BUT WHAT ELSE CAN I DO?

...IS IN CRITICAL CONDITION AT ST. VINCENT'S HOSPITAL. OFFICER MARSHA COLLINS IS PHYSICALLY UNHARMED BUT IN A DEEP STATE OF SHOCK AFTER--

IT'S BEEN WEEKS SINCE PETER DISAPPEARED. HE WOULDN'T JUST LEAVE LIKE THAT WITHOUT TELLING ME.

WHICH MEANS HE'S EITHER DEAD (NO, HE CAN'T BE DEAD! HE CAN'T!), OR--

DAILY BUGLE
SPIDER-MAN BERSERK!
SPIDER-MAN GOES ON AND ON MAYHEM A

KNOK KNOK

ONE O'CLOCK IN THE MORNING?

KNOK KNOK

OKAY, I'M COMING!

MARY JANE...?

I KNOW IT'S LATE, MR. ROBERTSON--

JOE. AND COME IN--

-- YOU LOOK LIKE DEATH WARMED OVER.

I DIDN'T MEAN--

GEE, THANKS.

I KNOW YOU DIDN'T, JOE, I'M SORRY. IT'S JUST THAT--

SIT DOWN, MARY JANE. CAN I GET YOU--

NOTHING, THANK YOU.

WHY DID I COME HERE?

BECAUSE JOE ROBERTSON IS THE EDITOR OF THE DAILY BUGLE? BECAUSE HE'S KNOWN PETER FOR YEARS? BECAUSE HE'S A MAN OF INTELLIGENCE AND INTEGRITY?

OR BECAUSE--

M.J.-- WHAT *IS* IT? IS SOMETHING WRONG WITH PETER?

MR. ROBERT-- JOE. I...

THERE'S SOMEONE OUT THERE. AND EITHER HE'S *NOT PETER*-- OR PETER'S GONE *INSANE.* EITHER WAY, I --

...I...

I CAN'T TELL HIM.

I'M SORRY I BOTHERED YOU. I REALLY SHOULDN'T HAVE COME HERE. IT WAS NOTHING.

NOTHING? YOU'RE SHAKING! AND YOU'RE--

REALLY. IT WAS NOTHING.

I'M SORRY. I'M VERY SORRY.

BUT, MARY JANE--

*BYE.*

EVEN IF HE DOES KNOW--

-- I CAN'T TELL HIM.

SPIDER-MAN GOES BERSERK!

DAILY BUGLE

KRA-
KOOM!

CHUK

CHUK

-- tonight.

I feel the herbs, the roots, the potions spreading wide my mind.

CHUK

Feel them reaching out to touch--

--*Destiny.*

CHUK

The newspapers call him...*it*... the "Cannibal Killer."

But *I* know it by name. I am the *HUNTER*; I know all beasts intimately.

I am *inside* you, Vermin; can you hear my call?

*Don't resist:* Let Destiny take our hands; draw us closer together.

I *understand* now--

--that there must be a *test*.

A final line to cross. A final madness embraced.

And only when I have tested, crossed, embraced will my victory over Spider-Man be complete; will my *honor* be *restored*.

You are my test, Vermin. My fire of *purification*.

Don't fear me.

*Love* me.

For I intend to *bless* you.

With pain. And blood. And sorrow.

*Tonight.*

TONIGHT.

SPLISH

SPLISH

SPLISH SPLISH

dreamdreamdream. *bad* dream. sssomeone calling me. chasing me.

but i'm home now. sssafe now. i'm--

SPLISH

SPLISH

SPLISH SPLISH

oh, no.

it wasssn't a dream! it wasss real! he wasss real!

and he'sss coming--

--to--

*akkk*

SKREEEE!!

HELLO, VERMIN. REMEMBER ME?

SSSPIDER-MAN.

YESSS.

BUT *I* DEFEATED YOU, DIDN'T I?

REMEMBER THE LAST TIME WE MET--HOW YOU ALMOST DEFEATED ME?

NO! NOT FAIR! YOU WEREN'T ALONE! YOU HAD CAPTAIN FLAG WITH YOU! YOU--

YOU

WEREN'T

ALONE!

But *I* can.

Dishonored Father. Sainted Mother.

Stained honor.

I

can!

I am the Spider-- and I know.

I see *into* things: *beyond* things. I see the strands of Fate that bind us: victims to victors.

In ways normal men cannot: *I know.*

I AM THE SPIDER.

And I rise up from the lower depths triumphant.

Up.

From.

The depths.

Triumphant.

MARY JANE...?

# CHAPTER

# 4

# RESURRECTION

WARM.

WHITE.

PEACEFUL.

NO! I DON'T **KNOW** ANYONE NAMED NED LEEDS!

*DEAD?*

I NEVER **HEARD** OF PETER PARKER!

*OH*

I JUST WANT TO BE LEFT **ALONE**--

*GOD*

-- IN THE WARM--

*HE'S*

-- WHITE--

*RIGHT.*

--PEACE--

--AND--

--QUIET.

Come out.

come out

come out

come
out

come out

come
out.

come
out

come out

come out

come

come out

come out

MARY JANE?

85

HOW LONG HAVE I *BEEN* THIS POWER? THIS *BEAST*? THIS CRAWLING, ALL-CONSUMING *THING*?

HOW LONG HAVE I *SEEN* THROUGH THE SPIDER'S EYES? DONE THE SPIDER'S BIDDING? WEAVED THE SPIDER'S WEB?

I AM THE *SPIDER*?

IS THAT *REALLY* WHO I AM?

YES. OF COURSE. THE SPIDER'S STRONG. FEARLESS. THE SPIDER CAN WIN. NOT LIKE--

*I*

--THAT *WEAKLING*.

*AM*

THAT *COWARD*.

I AM

THE ONE WHO CAN *DIE*.

*I AM PETER PARKER!*

THE **SPIDER'S** DYING! THE SPIDER NEVER **LIVED!** THE SPIDER'S A TRAP! A LIE!

A COFFIN!

AND I'VE GOT TO BE **FREE** OF IT.

I.

FREE.

I'M PETER PARKER.

THAT'S ALL I EVER WAS; ALL I EVER **WILL** BE.

AND I'M **GOING** TO BE FREE. YOU CAN'T **STOP** ME. YOU CAN'T **KEEP** ME HERE.

YOU'VE MURDERED A **MASK**, BUT YOU HAVEN'T MURDERED A **MAN**.

Come out

come out

come out

come out

come out

come out

come out

come out

come out

come out

ALL THESE YEARS YOU'VE MISUNDERSTOOD ME.

YOU THOUGHT I WAS SOMETHING LARGER THAN LIFE.

YOU THOUGHT I WAS MAGIC.

YOU THOUGHT I WAS MADNESS.

SOME CREATURE THAT CRAWLED AND SPUN AND HID IN SHADOWS, THAT MOCKED AND TORMENTED AND REVELED IN DARKNESS.

IDIOT!

THERE IS NO SPIDER!

( MARY JANE ?)

THERE'S JUST ME!

MARY JANE, I'M COMING!

JUST A NORMAL GUY -- WHO GOT TAPPED ON THE SHOULDER BY FATE.

MARY JANE, I LOVE YOU!

JUST PETER PARKER: THAT'S MY WEAKNESS.

THAT'S MY STRENGTH.

COME--

--OUT.

THAT'S...

COME OUT--

OH, **PLEASE**, GOD, DON'T LET IT HAPPEN AGAIN. I'VE GOT TO SEE HER. TOUCH HER. **LOVE** HER.

--SO I CAN **KILL** YOU--

MARY JANE-- YOU'VE GOT TO **HELP** ME! DON'T **LEAVE** ME HERE! DON'T LET ME **LOSE** YOU!

--AGAIN.

SPIDER!

MARY

THERE IS NO SPIDER!

JANE

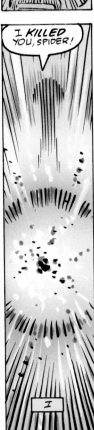

I **KILLED** YOU, SPIDER!

I

THERE **IS** NO SPIDER!!

LOVE

AND I'M GOING TO **KEEP** KILLING YOU-- OVER AND OVER AND OVER AND OVER AND OVER AND--

YOU!

89

CANNIBAL KILLER GULS

CRAZY IN

POLICE IN CITY

CANNIBAL KILLER ASSAULT!

COPS ATTACKED

NEW YORK TIMES

POLICE SKETCH

DAILY BUGLE

SPIDER-MAN BERSERK!

TWO

WEEKS?!?

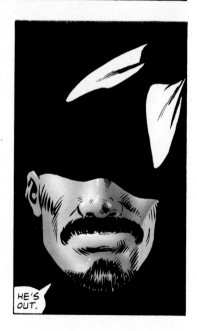

HE'S OUT.

TWO WEEKS!!

IN THE GROUND! IN THE GRAVE! DEAD!

TWO WEEKS!!

AND WHILE I'VE BEEN LYING THERE...TRAPPED...YOU'VE BEEN OUT THERE, KRAVEN-- WEARING MY COSTUME!

ABUSING MY NAME!

USURPING MY LIFE!!

TWO WEEKS!!

WHAT DID YOU SHOOT ME WITH, HUNTER? NOT BULLETS THAT'S FOR SURE. ONE OF YOUR JUNGLE POTIONS OR ROOTS OR WHATEVER YOU USE!

SHOOT ME UP... LAY ME DOWN... AS GOOD AS DEAD... A ZOMBIE... IN THE GRAVE!

OH, GOD... IN THE GRAVE!

TWO WEEKS!!

IN THE GRAVE.

93

AND WHILE I WAS ROTTING DOWN THERE... WHAT WAS MY *FAMILY* THINKING? AUNT MAY... MARY JANE...

MARY JANE... MY *WIFE.*

MY WIFE... MY LIFE!

TWO WEEKS!

I THINK I'M GONNA BE *SICK.*

NO. NOT YET.

< YOU WERE RIGHT. IT *IS* HIM. >

< I... UH... THINK WE SHOULD GET *OUT* OF HERE. >

< WHY? *LOOK* AT HIM. HE'S *WEAK.* HE CAN HARDLY--->

NOT.

< UH- OH. >

YET.

**WHERE?!**

WHERE?

LOOK AT THEM: THEY'RE TERRIFIED. THEY THINK I'M GOING TO KILL *THEM.* AND A PART OF ME WANTS TO. WANTS TO TEAR THEM APART TO GET BACK AT HIM.

BUT IT'S A VERY SMALL PART.

I'LL FIND KRAVEN. I'LL DEAL WITH HIM.

BUT NOT LIKE A SPIDER.

KRASSH

LIKE A MAN.

HE'S--

--COMING.

WHAT CAN IT HAVE *BEEN* LIKE FOR YOU? WAITING. WONDERING.

KNOWING THAT THERE WAS SOMEONE... A *LUNATIC* ...OUT THERE. SOMEONE WHO CALLED HIMSELF SPIDER-MAN. A *KILLER*.

A KILLER WHO MIGHT JUST BE YOUR *HUSBAND*.

SO YOU READ THE PAPERS. YOU WATCH THE NEWS. YOU DON'T SLEEP MUCH. YOU *CRY*.

KNOWING YOU, YOU PROBABLY WALK THE STREETS *LOOKING* FOR ME.

I PRAY TO GOD YOU DIDN'T *FIND* ME. *HIM*.

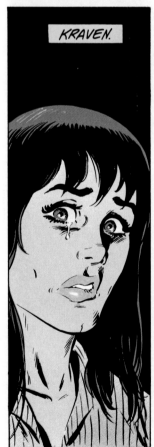

KRAVEN.

TWO WEEKS, MARY JANE. TWO WEEKS OF MY LIFE... *OUR* LIFE... OUR *NEW* LIFE TO-GETHER AS MAN AND WIFE.

*STOLEN* FROM US. TAINTED.

*DEFILED.*

THWIP

I *LOVE* YOU, MARY JANE.

MORE THAN I EVER *REALIZED*.

98

PETER...?

I LOVE YOU.

TRAPPED. AN ANIMAL. DEAD. IN THE GROUND IN THE GRAVE. MARY JANE! TWO WEEKS.

I THOUGHT I WAS *BACK* THERE. *DOWN* THERE. I THOUGHT...

MARY JANE...?

I'M IN THE *BATHROOM*, HON.

SHE'S *HERE*. THANK GOD. SHE'S *HERE*.

PETER -- WHAT ARE YOU *DOING*? GET BACK IN *BED*!

I'VE GOT TO *GO*.

YOU'RE NOT GOING *ANYWHERE*! YOU CAN HARDLY STAND! YOU CAN HARDLY *TALK*!

VOICE'LL COME BACK SOON *ENOUGH*. VOCAL CHORDS JUST HAVE TO--

I DON'T *CARE* ABOUT YOUR VOICE! YOU'VE BEEN THROUGH A TRAUMATIC EXPERIENCE! *I'VE* BEEN THROUGH A TRAUMATIC EXPERIENCE!

AND I'M NOT LETTING YOU OUT OF MY *SIGHT* UNTIL--

MARY JANE... I DON'T *WANT* TO GO. *BELIEVE* ME -- I WANT TO STAY RIGHT HERE WITH YOU. WHERE IT'S *SAFE*. WHERE NOTHING BAD CAN *TOUCH* ME.

BUT DON'T YOU SEE? HE'S *OUT* THERE. HE'S *WAITING*. HE'S *MURDERED* IN MY NAME!

I'VE GOT TO GO!

HE'S--

--COMING.

He's here.

# CHAPTER

# 5

# THUNDER

A woman of rare breeding... true nobility... and a tender heart.

Driven out of Russia by the Trotskys and Lenins.

Driven to America where she was overwhelmed by the poverty. The filth. The utter *mundanity* of life here.

Finally locked away, like an animal: trapped. Abused. Terrified.

KRA·KOOOOM!

SSHAAAAKKKK

And my father, his spirit broken, allowed it.

And I, just a child, could only watch—as helpless as *she* was.

They said my mother was insane; that she took her own life: *They lied.*

107

Her life was *stolen* from her.

Stolen

by

The Spider.

KRAVEN!

SPIDER-MAN.

Oh, I see now; I *understand* in a way I never could before. This costumed adventurer called Spider-Man is just that: *a man*.

And yet *within* him is something *more*: something great. Something awful.

YOU'VE GONE *TOO FAR* THIS TIME, KRAVEN!

The *essence* of the demon that brought Russia to ruin.

YOU ROBBED ME OF *TWO WEEKS* OF MY *LIFE*, YOU ANIMAL!

The demon that destroyed my father; consumed my mother.

*TWO WEEKS!*

KRAKKK

The demon I have at long last--

--defeated.

**KOOOM**

Yes, yes... I hear you. I understand. It's almost time--

--but not yet. Not yet.

Not till my victory is complete. And it will only be complete--

I'M GOING TO MAKE YOU *HURT!* I'M GOING TO MAKE YOU *SUFFER!* I'M GOING TO--

--when *he* understands.

HIT ME AGAIN IF YOU LIKE, SPIDER-MAN. HIT ME A HUNDRED TIMES.

I WON'T RESIST. I WON'T FIGHT. THERE'S NO *REASON* TO FIGHT.

But he *doesn't* understand.

DON'T YOU SEE?

I'VE FINALLY *WON!*

 I "KILLED" YOU, SPIDER-MAN. BURIED YOU. AND *AFTER* I "KILLED" YOU--

 --I TOOK YOUR PLACE.

 YOU *DRUGGED* ME, KRAVEN-- THREW ME INTO A STATE *SIMULATING* DEATH--

 YOU COULD JUST AS WELL HAVE BEEN DEAD HAD I WISHED IT.

I ONLY ALLOWED YOU TO LIVE--

 --SO THAT YOU COULD *KNOW* THAT I "KILLED" YOU.

 THAT--IN DONNING YOUR COSTUME, IN *REPLACING* YOU-- I PROVED MYSELF IN ALL WAYS --

 --YOUR SUPERIOR.

The *man* is confused--but The Spider comprehends. I feel his awe... his reverence. His--

-- submission.

But it is part of the *dance*, part of the *plan*, for the man to comprehend as well.

So I'll *show* him the Truth. And, when we finally *share* it--

-- we'll both be free.

FOLLOW ME, SPIDER-MAN.

YOU EXPECT ME TO JUST--?!

YOU HAVE SPECIAL SENSES THAT WARN YOU OF DANGER-- SO YOU KNOW THAT THERE'S NO *TRAP* WAITING BELOW.

COME WITH ME.

He hesitates.

He comes.

What else CAN he do?

How *calm* I feel; how *peaceful*. As if something inside me-- some knot, some tangle of fear and anger and so much more-- has been finally *untied*.

All these years: fleeing Russia, suffocating in America, finding release... finding honor... in the jungle. *All* these years-- and I've never *known* peace or calm or that elusive thing called *happiness*.

But I feel as if I can know it now. That it's nearby. Just outside, perhaps-- hidden in the patter of the rain, the drum-beat of the thunder.

Peace, calm, happiness. An *ending*.

Soon.

*SHAKKKKK*

VERMIN?!

YES. YOUR OLD FOE, VERMIN.

THE NEWSPAPERS HAVE BEEN CALLING HIM "THE CANNIBAL KILLER."

BUT WE KNOW WHAT HE *REALLY* IS, DON'T WE? THE PERFECT FUSION OF MAN AND ANIMAL. A VILE, TORMENTED, BEAUTIFUL *BEAST*--

--THAT I HAVE BEATEN--

--AND CAPTURED.

I.

KOOOM

I COULD FEEL HIM OUT THERE, SPIDER-MAN... I COULD TOUCH HIS SOUL-- AND I KNEW WHAT ROLE HE HAD TO PLAY IN OUR LITTLE GAME.

OUT... OUT... PLEASSSSSSE LET ME OUT!

HE WAS THE FINAL TEST. THE FINAL PROOF.

YOU WERE UNABLE TO DEFEAT HIM ALONE. YOU AND CAPTAIN AMERICA COULD BARELY DO IT TOGETHER. BUT I DEFEATED HIM.

LOOK AT HIM-- A WHIMPERING, TERRIFIED, PATHETIC LITTLE... MOUSE.

AND I DID IT.

NO...DON'T BURN ME! DON'T HURT ME ANY MORE!

PLEASSSSE!

SHAKKKK

Crawling upward: The man filled with compassion for the cowering beast--

--the Spider delighting in Vermin's torment.

But, of course, all Vermin knows is that Spider-Man hunted... defeated... captured... *humiliated* him--

--and the very sight of that black costume... those white eyes--

--drives the little mouse wild.

FIRE FIREFIRE FIREFIRE FIREFIRE FIREFIRE FIREFIRE

SSSSPIDER-MAN!! OHNOOHNOOH *NO!*

--DON'T HURT ME *AGAIN!!*

So the man behind the mask does what he can to alleviate the mouse's pain--

--then skitters back down the wall--

--turning his rage upon *me.*

THWIP

SSSSHIKKK

As if *I* were to blame for all this. What a monumental *joke!*

It was in the *jungles* that I first began to understand the ways of the spirits and demons... of the ravenous Spider.

And tonight I finally see that even the man inhabited the Spider--

-- is ignorant--

KRAVEN!

-- of its devious ways!

I HAVE *HAD* IT WITH YOU, DO YOU *HEAR* ME? YOU THINK YOU CAN JUST TURN MY LIFE INSIDE OUT--

-- AND THEN STAND THERE *GRINNING* LIKE SOME BRAIN-DAMAGED *GORILLA?* WELL, YOU CAN'T!

Poor man: possessed by the entity responsible for human suffering... world chaos... and he doesn't even know it!

I was as naive once... before I left this corrupted excuse for civilization behind.

Before I found the honor and dignity I'd lost when my country... my parents... fell to The Spider--

-- in the primitive wilds of Africa.

Hear me, Spider; hear me, man:

Hear the bellow of the elephant; the roar of the lion --

-- the triumph of Kraven.

116

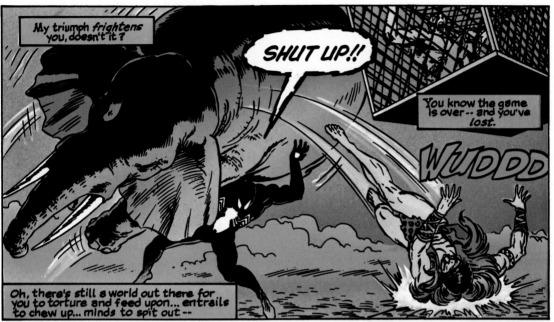

It's not enough to *display* the truth: the truth must be set free!

*Experienced* first-hand!

KRE AK

NOOOOO!

THIS... *THIS* IS THE FINALE, SPIDER-MAN!

YOU EXPECT ME TO *FIGHT* WITH HIM, *DON'T* YOU? FIGHT-- FOR YOUR *AMUSE-MENT!*

NO. FOR MY *EMANCIPATION.*

WELL, I WON'T DO IT!

PLEASSSSSE-- DON'T HITMEHURTME HITMEHURTMEHITME!

You won't have to.

VERMIN-- THIS IS YOUR CHANCE! SPIDER-MAN BEAT YOU DOWN... HURT YOU IN A WAY YOU'VE *NEVER* BEEN HURT BEFORE!

DON'T LET HIM GET *AWAY* WITH IT! DON'T LET HIM THINK HE'S BETTER... *STRONGER* THAN YOU ARE!

HURT HIM *BACK,* VERMIN! YOU OWE IT TO YOURSELF... TO *ALL* OF US!

HURT HIM *BACK!*

ROWWRRR

Hurt him, Vermin.

VERMIN -- *DON'T!* HE'S USING YOU! MAKING A *FOOL* OF YOU!

LIAR!!

YOU -- *YOU* MADE A FOOL OF ME!!

And, in hurting him... in *defeating* him--

NO VERMIN-- IT WASN'T *ME!* IT WAS KRAVEN-- IN MY COSTUME.. MIMICKING MY POWERS!

LIAR!

SHH-RAKK!

-- you'll make him see.

I'M GONNA TEAR YOU *UP!* I'M GONNA RIP OUT YOUR *HEART!*

I "killed" the Spider; I became the Spider; I vanquished the one foe the Spider *couldn't.*

All the years; all the shame.

KRA-

KOOM

*Erased.*

NO, VERMIN! I'M *NOT GOING* TO--

YARRGH!

SHOKK

Honor -- so long sought... so long elusive -- will be *restored.*

How old I suddenly feel.

ALL RIGHT, IF THAT'S THE WAY YOU *WANT* IT--

How unutterably tired.

--THAT'S THE WAY IT'S GONNA *BE!*

*KRAKK!*

The game was a good one; man to Spider... Spider to man--

--but it was so very, very long.

THAT'S THE WAY IT'S GONNA *BE!!*

*KRA-*

*KOOM*

They said my mother --

He *SHOT* ME... He *BURIED* ME! *BURIED* ME!

DO YOU KNOW WHAT THAT'S *LIKE,* YOU STUPID, DISGUSTING *ANIMAL!*

*SPAKKK!*

DO YOU KNOW WHAT THAT'S *LIKE?!*

120

NO.

KRAA KOOM

GARRRRRRR

KRAK-

KOOOM

KRAK-

-- was insane.

KOOOM

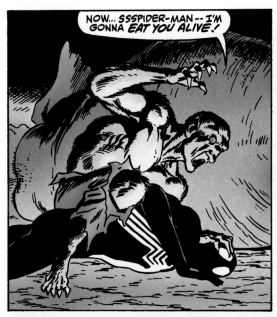

HE'S... HE'S KILLED BEFORE... HE'LL KILL AGAIN...!

*No matter.*

KRASH!

The Spider is alive in him; there will undoubtedly be others to rise up in opposition.

But it's no longer my concern.

LET ME HELP YOU...

*My Spider is gone. Now-- there's only a man.*

PLASH! PLASH!

*A good man, I think. How strange that I haven't been able to see that till now!*

*No matter.*

I do see; and seeing, Spider-Man, I thank you. And I bless you.

*If one such as Kraven can give blessings...*

KRAVEN... I I DON'T UNDERSTAND...

124

And there's one *final* thing I see; something I don't think I was capable of seeing 'till now: *every man has his Spider.* And perhaps I--

YOU'RE FREE. GO.

JUST LIKE THAT? GO?

A MAN LIKE YOU WON'T LET VERMIN RUN LOOSE. *GO.* FOLLOW YOUR CONSCIENCE.

AFTER ALL YOU'VE DONE, DO YOU THINK I'M *REALLY* GONNA--

*-- I have been YOURS.*

GO--WHILE *YOU* GO MERRILY ALONG...HUNT-ING...RUINING LIVES... *USING* PEOPLE TO--

AFTER ALL THESE YEARS, YOU SURELY KNOW THAT I'M A MAN OF MY WORD--

--AND I *GIVE* YOU MY WORD: FROM THIS NIGHT FORWARD, KRAVEN THE HUNTER--

-- WILL NEVER HUNT AGAIN.

I'LL BE *BACK!*

I don't doubt it.

Every man.... every woman... every nation... every Age has its Spider. You have been mine. What a burden. What an--

-- honor.

Goodbye.

How *calm* I feel; how *peaceful*. As if something inside me-- some knot, some tangle of fear and anger and so much more, has been finally *untied*.

All these years: fleeing Russia, suffocating in America, finding release... *finding honor*... in the jungle. All these years-- and I've never known peace or calm or that elusive thing called *happiness*.

But I feel as if I can know it now. That it's nearby. Just outside, perhaps-- hidden in the patter of the rain, the drum-beat of the thunder.

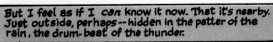

Peace, calm, happiness. An *ending*.

NOW.

KRA KOOOM

127

KRA

They said my mother was insane.

KOOOM

# CHAPTER

# 6

# ASCENDING

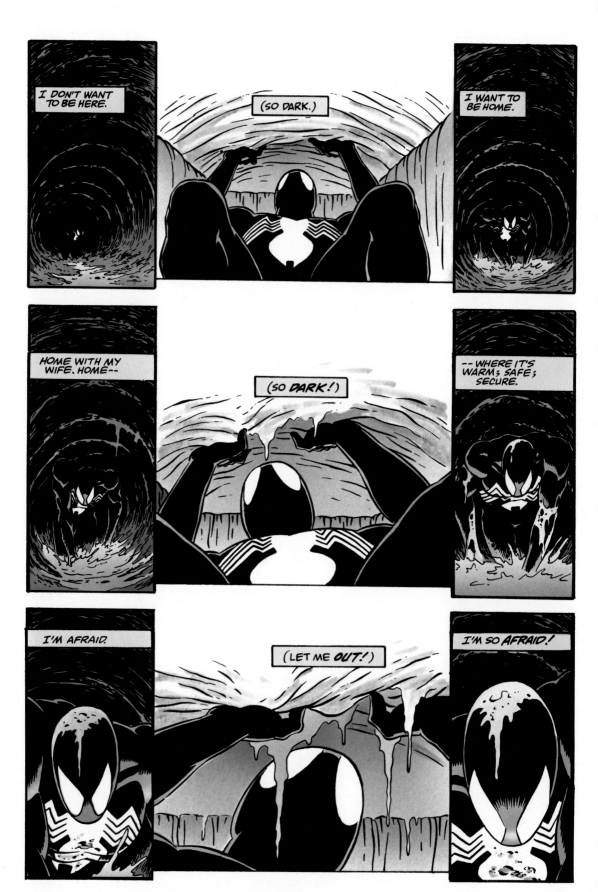

THE WORST OF IT IS OVER.

(I'M NOT DEAD!)

KRAVEN'S DEMENTED GAME: DRUGGING ME--

--BURYING ME ALIVE.

(I'M NOT DEAD!!)

OH, BUT DOWN *HERE*...IT FEELS SO MUCH LIKE IT DID WHEN I WAS--

SHUK

NO. THIS ISN'T A COFFIN...IT'S A SEWER. NO ONE'S LOCKED ME *AWAY*... I'VE COME DOWN HERE BECAUSE I WANT TO--

(I DON'T WANT TO BE HERE!)

-- BECAUSE I *HAVE* TO.

BECAUSE VERMIN'S HERE.

I CAN'T LET HIM RUN LOOSE; HE'S A KILLER! HE'S NOT *HUMAN!* HE--

(LET SOME-BODY *ELSE* CATCH HIM!)

-- EATS PEOPLE!

THESE PAST WEEKS, WHILE I'VE BEEN... *DEAD?*...

(I'M *NOT* DEAD!!)

...HE'S BEEN OUT ON THE STREET HUNTING... FEEDING. AND, KRAVEN--

NO!

HOW DOES HE *DO* IT? MAKE THEM OBEY HIM LIKE THAT? HE'S NOT HUMAN, IS HE? HE'S SOME KIND OF--

STOP IT! *STOP!* I KNOW HE'S HUMAN.' I'VE READ THE *FILES* ON HIM.'

HE WAS JUST A *MAN,* ONCE. UNTIL *BARON ZEMO* EXPERIMENTED ON HIM.

KRAK

MUTATED HIM INTO--

(-- INTO THE DARKNESS.')

-- SOME KIND OF *MAN-RAT.*

I AM NOT AFRAID. I AM NOT AFRAID. I AM NOT AFRAID.

YES, I AM.

BUT THERE'S NOTHING *WRONG* WITH THAT. NOTHING WRONG -- AS LONG AS I DON'T TURN BACK. AS LONG AS I DO WHAT'S *RIGHT.*

SHUK

...DETECTIVE CARSON?

YO.

THAT ANONYMOUS CALLER SURE WAS RIGHT, HUH? THIS PLACE--

-- SURE DID BELONG TO KRAVEN.

SEEMS THAT WAY.

LOT MORE THAN "SEEMS"... SIR. WE FOUND SOMETHING.

WHAT?

LOOKS T'ME LIKE A CONFESSION.

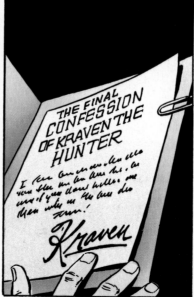

THE FINAL CONFESSION OF KRAVEN THE HUNTER

Kraven

AND QUITE A CONFESSION IT IS, BRODSKY.

139

PLOOOSH!

(I'M NOT DEAD!)

SPLOSH!

PLOOSS!

(I'M NOT DEAD!)

BUT WHAT IF I AM?

SMAKT

GRRRRRR

WHAT IF IT WASN'T A DRUG? WHAT IF I NEVER CAME UP? WHAT IF I'M STILL DOWN THERE? WHAT IF I REALLY AM--

POOTCH!

(I'M NOT--)

SPLOOSH

141

SSSPIDER-MAN...?

WHERE ARE YOU?

YOU-- YOU CAN'T HIDE FROM ME! I'LL FIND YOU! I'LL--

WHERE ARE YOU?!

YOU'RE NOT GONNA HITMEHURTMEHITMEHURT ME AGAIN!

YOU'RE NOT!

E-EVERYBODY HITSSSMEHURTSSS ME! EVERYBODY!

WHY WON'T THEY JUST LEAVE ME ALONE?

IT'S NOT MY FAULT THAT I GET HUNGRY ISSS IT?

OH, HE'SSS HERE, SOMEWHERE... I JUSSST KNOW IT!

AND HE'SSS GOING TO HITMEHURTME-- ALL OVER AGAIN!

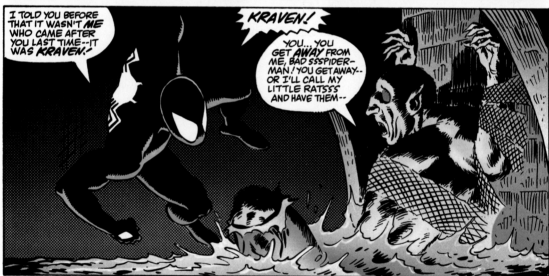

REMEMBER: HE DIDN'T **ASK** FOR THIS. **ZEMO** DID THIS TO HIM! THERE'S A **MAN** BURIED IN THERE--

I WON'T I WON'T I **WON'T!**

( BURIED. )

--AND I'VE GOT TO FIND SOME WAY TO **STOP** HIM--

**LISTEN** TO ME, VERMIN--

( ALIVE! )

-- AND **HELP** HIM!

-- I DON'T WANT TO HURT YOU! **I** DON'T!

NO...?

NO!

I WANT TO **STOP** YOUR HURT!

OOOO, THAT WOULD BE **NICCCE.**

I WANT TO TAKE YOU **UP**--

NO MORE HIT AND HURT AND **HURT** HIT AND **HURT...**

-- OUT OF THE **DARKNESS**--

OUT OF THE **DARKNESS**--

**NO!**

**SNAP!**

**CHUD**

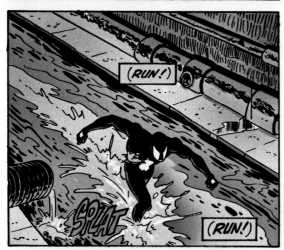

148

HONK! HONK!

INTO THE LIGHT.

THAT'S HIM, ISN'T IT? THAT'S OUR "CANNIBAL KILLER"!

WE'LL NEED BACK-UP... LOTS OF IT!

SO BRIGHT... SO BRIGHT!!

I DON'T THINK SO.

TAKE IT AWAYAWAY AWAY!

PLEASSSE TAKE THE LIGHT AWAY...?

THWIP

LISTEN TO 'IM! HE'S-- WHIMPERIN' LIKE A-- LIKE A PUPPY!

ROO ROO ROOO

VERMIN-- THERE'S A MAN I'M GOING TO CALL... HIS NAME'S REED RICHARDS.

IF ANYBODY CAN HELP YOU-- HE CAN.

NO! I DON'T WANT YOUR HELP! I DON'T!

KREEK

PETER...?

PETER--YOU'RE HOME!

YOU'RE HOME!

I'M HOME.

Spyder! Spyder! burning bright

SHUK

In the forests of the night

SHUK

What immortal hand or eye

could frame thy fearful

symmetry?

# Afterword

## Setting the Stage

You know the story. In fact, ask almost anyone about Spider-Man's origin and that person will tell you: "He was bitten by a radioactive spider." The concept almost sounds ludicrous now because the general public is more aware of the potential effects of radiation than they were in the '60s. But you can't accuse Stan Lee and Steve Ditko of avoiding contemporary issues when they created the Amazing Spider-Man.

Many of Marvel's early creations were products of radioactivity. Society was experiencing a growing concern about the possible consequences of radiation, and Stan Lee played upon these fears. While popular horror films of that era dealt with such themes as radioactive ants growing thousands of times their normal size, Stan and Steve brought the fear closer to home. Concerned with the common man, these men shied away from such ideas and proposed this concept: "What if a bookish teenager was suddenly given the powers of, say, a spider?"

Due to their concern with human frailty over the all-too-fantastic, Spider-Man became an instant success because so many fans could relate to him. After all, everyone knows what it's like attending high school, studying for exams, worrying about grades and relationships with the opposite sex. Many of us also understand what it's like trying to make the college grade or worrying about this month's rent.

We. still receive letters reading, "I've grown up with Spider-Man. I went to high school with him, I attended college the same time he did. Now he's married to a beautiful woman and so am I. We've experienced many of the same trials and triumphs. I feel as though I know him as a friend."

The greatest secret to Spider-Man's success was that Stan and Steve took an ordinary high school student named Peter Parker and granted him the added problem of super powers. Thus, for the first time in comic book history, a super hero's powers were as much a burden as they were a blessing.

Of course, Peter had to learn the immortal lesson that "with great power there must also come great responsibility." Unlike most heroes before him, Peter was not born with an inherent heroic ideal. Initially he used his powers for personal gain, first by entering the sport of professional wrestling, then later as a spectacular stunt performer on a network variety show. After the taping of one of those shows, however, a burglar ran by Spider-Man who irresponsibly allowed him to escape, although he could have easily stopped him. A few days later the same burglar murdered Peter's adopted father, his Uncle Ben. This discovery changed the course of Peter's life and he vowed that no one would be harmed due to Spider-Man's indifference again.

Because of this pledge, Peter began to use his powers to fight crime. He earned a living for himself and his Aunt May by selling photographs of himself in action to the *Daily Bugle*. Ironically, the newspaper's publisher, J. Jonah Jameson, had launched a campaign against the wall-crawler in his editorials. Thus, in addition to the villains he had to face on a seemingly daily basis, Spider-Man also had to contend with the negative publicity being generated about him.

The public's response again made Spider-Man unique in the world of heroes—he wasn't always perceived as a good guy by society and on several occasions he has been sought by the police as a criminal. In fact, Peter's own Aunt May fears his costumed alter ego.

Although Spider-Man remains a controversial figure, he has faced and thwarted a vast array of criminals and psychopaths in Manhattan, including Kraven the Hunter, who first appeared in AMAZING SPIDER-MAN #15, recently reprinted in MARVEL MASTERWORKS Vol. V. Through thick and thin, he has always remained a hero who is at his best even during the worst of times. Occasionally a little sunshine flickers into the woebegone web-slinger's life, such as his recent marriage to long-time sweetheart, Mary Jane Watson. However, a cloud of doom in the form of vengeful foes always seems to blow over the happiness. For soon after a pleasant honeymoon in Marseilles, France, Spider-Man confronts a manic Kraven—and loses.

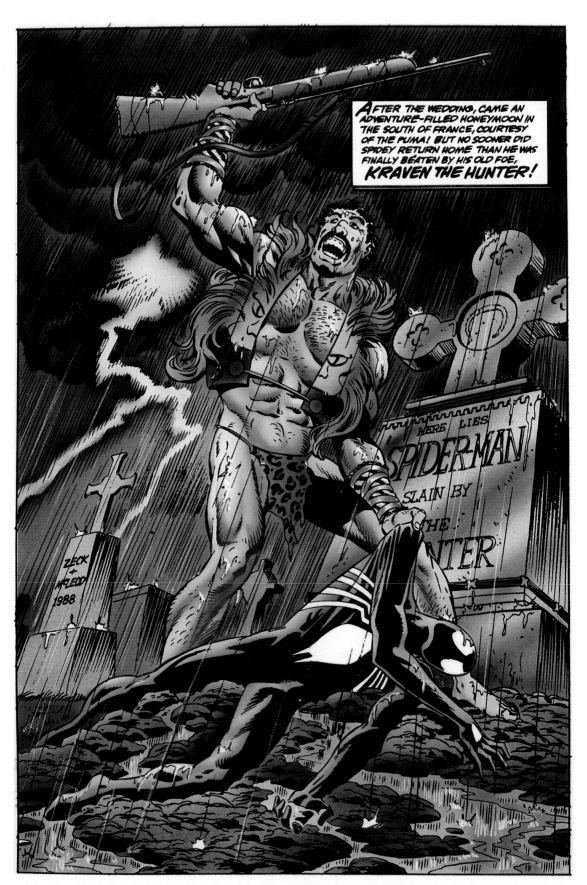

## Who, What, and Why?

J.M. DeMatteis, famed author of the MOON-SHADOW Limited Series from Epic Comics, proposed the controversial Kraven tale for then-Spider-Man editor Jim Owsley. DeMatteis wished to write a powerful tale that would reveal the timeless character of Spider-Man without needlessly "revamping" his origin. In fact, it was a response to the revamping of classic comic book characters at other companies that served as the impetus to create this story. Owsley wanted to prove the dogma that executive editor Mark Gruenwald is fond of preaching: "Marvel doesn't need to revamp their characters. We got them right the first time."

Mike Zeck, who garnered fan raves for his detailed work on SECRET WARS and the PUNISHER Limited Series, was selected to draw "Kraven's Last Hunt." And, of course, none other than Bob McLeod could complement Zeck's beautiful pencils with his precise inking style.

Jim Owsley originally planned to run the six-part tale in PETER PARKER, THE SPECTACULAR SPIDER-MAN. Then along came Jim Salicrup, the latest in a seemingly endless line of Spider-Man editors. Salicrup decided that he would run "Kraven's Last Hunt" through all three Spider-Man titles.

That's right, Spider-Man had become so popular over the years that the original Spidey title, THE AMAZING SPIDER-MAN, wasn't enough to contain him. Therefore, SPECTACULAR and WEB OF SPIDER-MAN were created to fill the demand. Unfortunately, the continuity among the titles never satisifed Salicrup.

So this new Spider-editor's first goal was to create a continuity so tight that an adventure in one Spider-Man title would lead directly into the next title. He initiated this plan with "Kraven's Last Hunt" because he felt the story would have a greater impact without any other Spider-Man stories simultaneously competing for attention. "After all," he argued, "if Spidey is buried alive by Kraven in one title, it wouldn't be all that logical having him battle Doctor Octopus next week in another title."

More importantly, Salicrup hoped to suspend disbelief in the story as much as possible by reinforcing that Spider-Man was *one* character, not three. Finally, by running the six parts across all three titles, fans wouldn't have to wait an entire month for the next installment, and a story that would have originally taken six months to unfold now took only two.

For the most part, the reaction was sensational. All across the nation these issues sold out, with SPECTACULAR and WEB selling as well as AMAZING for the first time. Mike Zeck's beautifully colored covers were so dramatic and powerful it seemed that no one could resist them. People who hadn't glanced at SPIDER-MAN in years picked up these issues!

Not only were these six issues a sales sensation, but they were critcially well-received as well. DeMatteis's tale of Kraven's obsessive desire to redeem his honor by finally defeating Spider-Man, and then taking his place received rave reviews from fans and critics alike.

But there was also an unforeseen response. We received almost 500 letters of complaint. Most were from subscribers who viewed our decision to run the story through all three titles as a cheap marketing ploy designed to make them purchase every title. In other words, subscribers who received just THE AMAZING SPIDER-MAN in their mailboxes only had a chance to witness the second and fourth parts of the saga. Some were so irate they canceled their subscriptions. Other subscribers rightfully complained that the reason they subscribed was due to a lack of comic book stores in their areas, and thus were unable to locate the missing parts.

Of course, this problem was not anticipated and we were caught off guard. Marvel had presented continued stories for years. Indeed, it was a Marvel trademark. And crossovers were not uncommon. Often stories would begin in one title and conclude in another. In recent years, following the success of SECRET WARS, it has virtually become an annual tradition to have multi-title crossovers as the big event of the year, and not only at Marvel!

We apologized and tried to make reparations to the offended parties. We also promised we'd avoid such tightly plotted crossovers without any recaps in the future. Recently, during the big Inferno tie-in, we managed to do a "crossover" throughout all three Spider-Man titles again, but in such a way that we have yet to receive a single complaint.

## To be or not to be

Of greater concern, however, and on a more serious note, was the quantity of letters we received castigating us for what some believed to be a glorified suicide in our comic, especially at a time when teenage suicide is at an all-time high. In fact, one outraged mother went so far as to accuse us of advocating suicide and referred to our comics as "destroying literature."

Again, the whole concern revolved around the storyline being divided into separately-sold parts, rather than the gestalt you are now holding (which the creators insist they originally intended it to be). Taken out of context, that issue might look as though we were advocating suicide. As a matter of fact, when editor in chief Tom DeFalco invited DeMatteis to read part V separately, the writer suddenly understood how his story could be misunderstood. Narrated by the deranged Kraven, it explained how he chose to die what he considered a "noble" death rather than sit around waiting to die "dishonorably" from old age. After all, his life had been prolonged by mystical formulas and he believed he had accomplished his life's goal. Once he "killed" the Spider, his most elusive prey, there was no reason for the Hunter to go on living.

DeMatteis realized that another story was needed to illuminate the confusion concerning Kraven's death. Since then he has plotted that story, and Mike Zeck and Bob McLeod will once again illustrate this eulogy that will clearly demonstrate to one and all that Kraven's actions were not those of a sane man—that suicide was just a sad conclusion to a sad and wasted life.

## But should fantasy deal with realism?

This conflict introduces the notion of whether "real-life" themes should be dealt with in the context of a fantasy world. Many people wrote us expressing their views that Spider-Man is a children's character who shouldn't be involved with such intense story-lines. One would infer that they believe everything about the wall-crawler should be candy-coated and totally escapist. We, on the other hand, feel that anyone who believes such nonsense doesn't understand who Spider-Man is or what he represents.

From the very outset, SPIDER-MAN explored mature themes. Peter's desire to selfishly exploit his powers led to his allowing the escape of the man who would later kill his uncle. Since most Spider-Man fans are completely familiar with that story from repeated readings, the dramatic impact might have subsided. But think about it. Is the story of a teenager responsible for the death of his surrogate father typical escapist fare?

Spider-Man has also been involved with stories dealing with child molesting and drug abuse. In fact, the Comics Code Authority refused to put their seal of approval on a series of stories dealing with Harry Osborn's experimentation with LSD. But Marvel saw it as too important a story not to see print and it shipped without the seal.

The recurring theme of "with great power there must also come great responsibility" has been Spider-Man's major motivation since the beginning. Likewise, we have always taken great responsibility in what we present in these stories. Indeed, it was a reaction to the irresponsible "new-age hero" who is becoming so popular that inspired the genesis of this six-parter.

Donning the mantle of Spider-Man, Kraven becomes a distorted hero, a twisted view that is now being passed off as true heroism in various "revamped" versions of classic comic book characters. Although themes of violence and revenge dominate FEARFUL SYMMETRY, the overriding motive of responsibility is never lost on Spider-Man,

only questioned. Spider-Man is a hero *despite* his power, not because of it. Whereas Spider-Man has learned to resist the awful temptations his power presents, Kraven completely gives into it when he assumes the role. Such themes should not be discarded or treated cynically. To do so would be irresponsible.

## From Fairy Tales to MARVEL TALES

Dealing with the themes we have discussed in such a manner as we have presented in this opus is a way of communicating important ideas to children (as well as adults) in a form that they can understand. Such forms go all the way back to Grimm's Fairy Tales (in their original form, not the censored, rehashed candy-coated tripe you read in the Little Golden Book versions). Scholars and psychologists are beginning to see what many of us have known for ages, that learning through such forms has greater value than what a child might learn in a text book. In fact, many school systems are using simulated comic books as teaching aids. And some colleges and universities offer courses in comic books and in fairy tale literature.

In his book, *The Uses of Enchantment* (Vintage Books, 1977), Dr. Bruno Bettelheim argues convincingly that fairy tales provide a unique way for children to cope with the predicaments of their inner lives. However, he notes one crucial limitation: "The true meaning and impact of a fairy tale can be appreciated, its enchantment can be experienced, only from the story in its original form." If we had chosen to discard the suicide scene in FEARFUL SYMMETRY, the story would have lost most of its underlying theme and mystery, even if Kraven had died some other way.

Many of our fans defended us from the accusations made by other letter-writers. One wrote the following: "Children will sooner or later be introduced to suicide and its devastating effects on family, friends, and others. If parents cannot educate them and discuss the topic and find it necessary to

put down a mere comic book trying to write a simple story, then I think there are some children out there who may receive a great shock in the world."

Another defender wrote: "If kids read SPIDER-MAN and see how bad an effect suicide has on loved ones or see that other choices are available, they may change their minds and go with one of the other choices."

Other people brought up the occurrences of suicide in Shakespeare and denounced the attitude of sheltering children from the cold hard facts. One wrote that "this attitude of 'ignore it, it'll go away' is the real problem in our society."

Yes, such themes are as old as the first fairy tales that were taught by word of mouth, but they are still found in such popular fantasy stories as STAR WARS and STAR TREK.

Obviously, Spider-Man has a deep root in people's hearts. The important thing to remember is that the real Spider-Man does not give up, even though he is tempted. He literally crawls back from the grave to tackle life's problems while it's the crazed Kraven who embraces death.

Spider-Man is a hero. But he is first and foremost human, and as such he sometimes makes mistakes. We at Marvel are also human and just as capable of making mistakes. But we don't give up. We're constantly trying to create stories that are entertaining yet true to our characters. Along with the current creative teams, writers David Michelinie and Gerry Conway, artists Todd McFarlane, Sal Buscema, Alex Saviuk and Keith Williams, letterer Rick Parker, and colorist Bob Sharen, we are dedicated to producing work of which we can all be proud. We hope that all of you are just as proud.

*—Glenn Herdling*
*and Jim Salicrup*

# About the Creators

Photo by Wendy Cahn.

J.M. DeMatteis was born in Brooklyn, New York on December 15, 1953.

He has written for newspapers, magazines, television, and, of course, comics where he's best known for his work on DC Comics' popular JUSTICE LEAGUE titles, and his groundbreaking graphic novels, MOONSHADOW, BLOOD: A TALE, and GREENBERG, THE VAMPIRE, all published by Marvel/Epic.

We think DeMatteis is still living in upstate New York, but, with him, you never know.

Photo by Reneé Witterstaetter

Mike Zeck grew up in south Florida splitting his days between going to school because he had to and drawing super heroes because he wanted to. This led him to spend his college years at Ringling School of Art in Sarasota, Florida, where he could do both at the same time.

Then followed a few years of laid-back Ft. Lauderdale beach life before Mike became aware that he wasn't independently wealthy and would need a career in this lifetime. So he set out to make his hobby his career and began showing his portfolio to the various comic book companies in New York.

During the summer of 1975, Mike started receiving assignments from Charlton publications until their comics line folded in 1977. Since then he has worked virtually full time for Marvel Comics including long stints on MASTER OF KUNG FU, CAPTAIN AMERICA, SECRET WARS, and THE PUNISHER.

**Bob McLeod**
Born: 8/9/51 in Tampa, Florida.
Attended Auburn University and the Art Institute of Fort Lauderdale.
First Job: "Westworld" satire for CRAZY Magazine (1974).
Credits: CONAN, SPIDER-MAN, STAR WARS, SUB-MARINER, X-MEN, etc. Co-created THE NEW MUTANTS.
Influences: Neal Adams, Mort Drucker, Tom Palmer, Stan Drake, John Buscema.
Current Work: THE SAGA OF THE SUB-MARINER Limited Series and THE NEW TITANS (DC).